DOMINIC GROWS
• SWEETCORN •

Written by Mandy Ross
Illustrated by Alison Bartlett

FRANCES LINCOLN
CHILDREN'S BOOKS

One Friday, after school, Dominic went for tea
at Grandad Wilford and Grandma Dora's.

"Mmm, sweetcorn-on-the-cob!"
said Dominic. "Yum!"
    "We used to grow sweetcorn, back in Jamaica,"
said Grandad. "Now I've stopped work, I'm going
to try growin' it here. You want to help, my boy?"
    "Yes please," said Dominic.

Next day, Dominic and Grandad Wilford
went out into the garden.
  "It looks like a jungle," groaned Dominic.
  Dominic and Grandad cleared and weeded
all weekend – and all the next weekend too.

"Grandad, what did you grow, back in Jamaica?" asked Dominic.

"We had lemon trees, orange trees, lime an' mangoes," said Grandad. "It was cool, high in the hills. Perfect for growing coffee."

"Coffee?" asked Dominic.

"Yes!" nodded Grandad. "We brewed our own fresh coffee. Mmm, I can smell it now. An' in the field behind the house, we grew sweetcorn."

"Much better!" said Grandad, when they'd cleared
the weeds. "Now we need to dig the soil to get the air in."
"Lots of worms," said Dominic, as he dug.
"I like to see the worms a-wigglin'," laughed Grandad.
"I remember the chickens used to come an' peck at them."

"Chickens?" asked Dominic.

"Yes, my boy!" laughed Grandad. "We children looked after the chickens. We collected the eggs before we went to school. An' we had pigs and goats, too, and a few cows. We drank the milk fresh and warm from the cow."

Next Saturday, round at Grandad's,
Dominic planted the seeds.
   "Two in each little pot," said Grandad.
   They put the pots on a sunny windowsill,
ready to get growing.

"Did you grow everything you needed in Jamaica?" asked Dominic.

"No, we'd trade," said Grandad. "Each week, a trader would come from the lowlands. He'd bring sugar cane, or cocoa, or jars of honey. The fishermen would bring baskets of fish to trade. We'd sell our lemons or mangoes in exchange. Then we'd brew some coffee and swap the news."

Two weeks later, the baby sweetcorn plants were sprouting.
   "Can we plant them out soon?" asked Dominic,
watering the row of pots.
   "When the weather's a bit warmer," said Grandad.
"Shall I tell you another story about Jamaica?"
   "Yes please."

"One time, when I was gettin' grown up," said Grandad,
"I saw a young girl coming, 'bout 17 years old.
'My dad's ill,' she said. 'I've brought the sugar cane to trade.'
Oh my, she was a pretty girl. I made sure to bring our
very best coffee," smiled Grandad. "An' that was how
I met your Grandma Dora."

 "Trading sugar cane!" smiled Dominic.

 Grandad nodded. "After a while, we wanted to get married.
But there was no work for us, there in Jamaica."

When the weather had warmed up a bit,
Dominic and Grandad planted the baby sweetcorn
plants out in the garden.

"I hope we grow enough sweetcorn to trade,"
smiled Dominic.

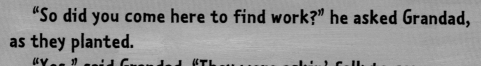

"So did you come here to find work?" he asked Grandad,
as they planted.

"Yes," said Grandad. "They were askin' folk to come
over here for all sorts of jobs, in the hospitals, on the buses.
Me and Grandma Dora, we made a plan.
We were going to get married, come and work
over here for five years, and then go back home."

"But you're still here!" laughed Dominic.

"Yes," said Grandad. "This is our home now."

"**Grandad!** Our sweetcorn's growing!" called Dominic,
next time he visited. "Shall I water them again?'"
"Yes, help them grow tall and strong," said Grandad.
"Just like you."

"Did you come to Britain by boat?" asked Dominic.
"No, by plane," said Grandad. "It was a long journey.
We came to stay with your great uncle Arthur,
who was over here already. We felt so cold when
we arrived! The first day we were too cold
to go outside, an' the next day, too."

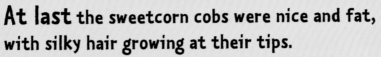

At last the sweetcorn cobs were nice and fat,
with silky hair growing at their tips.
　"Are they ripe?" asked Dominic.
　Grandad pulled opened the green leafy cover.
　"You press one of the seeds with your fingernail,
like this," he said. "See that milky juice comin' out?
That means they're ripe."
　Dominic and Grandad picked lots of fat cobs.

"Did you and Grandma Dora work hard?"
asked Dominic.

"Yes," sighed Grandad. "And harder still when the babies
came, your dad and his sisters. Grandma Dora looked after
them while I went to work. Then at night,
I'd see to the babies, an' your Grandma Dora worked nights
at the hospital. Work, work, work!"

"Sounds hard, Grandad," said Dominic.

"It was," smiled Grandad. "But now I can stay
at home an' look after my garden with you, my boy."

"Morning, Wilford!" called Jim, from over the fence.
"Morning, young Dominic! Do you want some tomatoes?
I've grown too many! We can't eat them all."
Dominic looked at Grandad and smiled.

"We'll trade!" said Dominic. "We'll give you some of our sweetcorn-on-the-cob in exchange!"

That afternoon, Dominic and Grandma Dora
made tomato salad, while Grandad Wilford
barbecued sweetcorn-on-the-cobs.
Then they invited Jim from
over the fence.

"What a garden feast we've grown!" smiled Grandad Wilford.
"And traded!" said Dominic. "Mmm... delicious!"

How to Make Sweetcorn Fritters

You can make these fritters with sweetcorn
cut from the cob, or from a tin of sweetcorn.
Makes about 10 fritters.

YOU WILL NEED
* 200g (1 cup) sweetcorn (tinned or cut from the cob)
* 2 spring onions or 1 red pepper chopped up small (optional)
* 75g (1/4 cup) self-raising flour
* 2 eggs, beaten
* 6 tablespoons milk
* Pinch of salt and pepper
* 2 tablespoons vegetable oil for frying

1. Mix egg, flour, salt and pepper.

2. Gradually stir in milk to make a smooth batter.

3. Stir in the sweetcorn (and spring onion or red pepper
if using them).

4. Heat shallow oil in a frying pan.

5. When the oil is hot, drop in a spoonful of the mixture
for each fritter. Fry for two or three minutes on each side
till golden.

6. Serve hot or cold.

Background to the Story

Over the years, people have moved from the Caribbean to live
and work in many other countries. In the 1950s and 1960s,
Britain needed more workers. They invited workers to come
from countries which had been part of the British Empire,
including Jamaica. Many people came and settled
from the Caribbean – just like Dominic's grandparents.